White Valentine

Michèle Laframboise

White Valentine

A WOW romance

Echofictions

Cover design by Echofictions
Original picture © Shutterstock /Chonnanit
Author portrait © Gilles Gagnon
Interior illustrations by the author

This book published by : Echofictions
Mississauga, Ontario

www.echofictions.com

ISBN 978-1-988339- 48-1 (print)

Table of contents

for Kris Kathryn Rusch,
with my thanks

White Valentine

NICK LEANED ON THE STEERING WHEEL, squinting hard through the quickly freezing windshield. Two rows of copy-paste bungalows dwindled away in a perfect one-point perspective, marked by the phantom glows of receding streetlights. Falling snow blurred the edges of the houses like a fuzzy picture on an old TV set.

A hostile wind blew through cracks and cavities, its teasing whistle putting a lie to the hermetic bubble his 2019 Volvo should be. Cold was also creeping in, making Nick regret the warm duffel coat he had left at home. His thin grey Takay nylon vest was no more than a fashion statement.

He felt as tired and cold as the earth under the pavement. He loved the winter and snow, but only inside his fantasy novels.

His starched shirt pulled and stretched across his shoulders, his belt divided his body painfully into two unrelated parts. His feet were sore, despite the Superior Shoes vendor's assurance that his new ankle boots would "loosen up" quickly.

Lying on the passenger seat, the pink, heart-shaped chocolate box and the grocery store rose bouquet seemed to mock him. The yellow roses had many petals and no scent. Even if Nick bent close, he could only inhale the oily and rubbery new car smell.

His empty stomach growled, as he had been too nervous to eat. He had tried to stave off hunger with mints, but the last one had dissolved on his tongue an hour ago.

For a moment, Nick was tempted to roll into a tight ball under the emergency quilt, the snow falling over his metal burrow, sleeping like some innocent animal until the next spring… forgetting all about this ill-fated date. He was a computer geek, not James Bond.

The gushy female voice of the GPS had insisted he had the wrong address. Nick had parked at the curb of the nameless copy-paste neighborhood to check on a five-year old paper map. As puffy flakes lined the wipers, slowly building upward, Nick realized that, in his eagerness, he had mixed up East and West Avenue.

When he inserted the key in the ignition, the six-cylinder engine did not roar to life. The sub-par battery had died, leaving him stranded.

And soon to be late, unforgettably late. The house numbers were in the unforgiving four-digit range. No way he could walk that distance as flimsily dressed as he was.

Nick looked at his Blackberry, wondering how long the AAA service he had called would take to reach him. A brand-new car, two months off the lot! There would be hell to pay, by someone else. He waited, the storm whispering and laughing around him.

By now, the snow palisade obscured the entire windshield.

જ•ન્

YOU'RE A NERVOUS WRECK, Dell told herself.

She was fretting and walking in tight circles around the clutter of furniture in her pocket-sized living room.

The clock ticked off the minutes, and no Nick Glass had appeared. She surveyed the two-room apartment, the best she could afford in this uppity part of the city. Scrubbed hardwood floors, counters and tidy dinner table, cutlery gleaming. No lingering, neglected vegetable odor. Her vegetable drawers regularly turned into moldering crypts.

The agency *No Lover Left Behind* had matched Dell with a male of her appropriate age and inclinations. Inclinations here meaning not too shabby, not too shiny.

The agency counselor, sporting three layers of eye make-up, had made her complete a questionnaire. The sparkling offices of the agency, and the hefty fee, had intimidated Dell.

"It's our Valentine Special", the woman (with some cloned-syllable name like Mimi or Lily) had said, juggling a toothpick between yellowing teeth.

Dell had signed her full name, her hand shaking, as if the entering a contract with the devil.

"De-li-lah," the cloned-syllable-named counselor had said. "Like in that Tom Jones song."

That the counselor even mentioned the singer betrayed her ripe age. Maybe the same age as her mother, who had

3

been a Tom Jones groupie when she named her first daughter.

Dell had let the lady take a bad digital photo of her best profile (the one not showing her scar.) Then she got out as fast as she could, fleeing the harsh new reality of the world.

❧

UNEXPECTEDLY, the phone had rung the day before yesterday.

"Er, is that Delilah-45?" a male voice had asked.

The voice was low and rumbling, hesitant.

Dell had instinctively made sure her raven hair fell over the left side of her face. Like a mysterious lady in those dime novels her father had loved to read. She gulped before answering in a voice as clear and light as she could make it.

"Are you... Nicholas-Twelve?"

The agency's idea of providing only the first name of your prospective date with a number had terrified Dell. The counselor had reassured her, then called a manager. A more-heavily made-up woman had come in and took five minutes of her obviously valuable time explaining the screening process.

"We don't let any perp or pervert into our system," she said, her gold bracelets clanking as she slashed the air with her right hand. All the time, her black rimmed eyes focused on the slanted red Y patch marring Dell's cheek.

❧

DELL INCHED NEAR THE WINDOW, not bending too much in her too-tight cocktail dress.

After giving Nicolas-Twelve, alias Nick Glass (it seemed that he didn't care for the numbering system any more than she did and had blurted out his name) the directions, she had spent the next 48 hours oscillating between depression and excitement, pretending not to notice the parade of red and rose chocolate boxes at the office, or the shops laden with flowers, or the occasional sorry glance cast in her direction.

One hand holding her mother's ivory pearl necklace, she peeked through the narrow gap in the closed curtains.

The street had become a white tableau with flurries that would have been welcome last December. In February, the promise of another morning of shoveling out the front alley daunted her.

She should have got out sooner to do the chore. But she had been too busy prepping herself in front of her bathroom mirror, trying every combination of foundation cream and powder to reduce the angry glare of the Y-shaped scar.

Dell had no real obligation to do the shoveling for the four-storey building. But one day when, coming back from work, she saw the eighty-year-old landlady trudging with a shovel as big as she was, the younger woman has stopped right then and there and offered to take care of the chore until Mrs. Elvina could find someone else.

Big fat flurries were landing on the rim of the stamp-sized balcony. Dell scanned the empty street, the parked cars slowly morphing into two lines of white hills.

The promised date was probably searching for a parking place, finding none. He would be trying another snow-filled street. Dell had become an expert at finding excuses for others' conduct.

Until reality bit her in the face.

He won't come.

The sentence filtered into her thoughts, followed by a host of like-minded friends.

The storm had been too much for him. Nick had spotted the small bump of the scar on the digital photograph. That's what had happened at the last agency. Dell had spent months dying inside before finding out. Yes, people were that shallow.

∽∽

DIALING THE WOMAN'S NUMBER took three attempts on the Blackberry. Nick was shivering in the freezing car as he pressed the buttons. The windshield was completely obscured by now; only the screen's bluish glow guided his fumbling fingers.

∽∽

THE PHONE RANG.

I knew it, Dell thought, clenching her fists.

Maybe it would be for the best, she told herself, looking at the laden table, the glasses waiting to be filled.

She swallowed up the ball of tears threatening to choke her. She was tempted not to answer but Nice Dell picked up the phone anyway. After all, she had paid the hefty agency fee. She couldn't back off now.

She steeled herself for the excuse, the expression of regrets.

"Hey, Delilah, its Aline," a familiar voice bubbled. "Are you doing something special this evening?"

Dell sighed. Her well-married little sister always chose the worst time to call.

"I have a date."

"Oh." Aline said, her voice conveying a truckload of emotion in one-syllable.

"He should be arriving any minute now," Dell said, her voice heavy.

"Does he know... *(Aline stopped herself in time.)* Well, I hope it goes well."

Aline knew the history of the scar.

Dell ended the conversation, noting the one minute and thirty-seven seconds of unavailability. She checked the missed call feature.

No one had called.

The guy was one hour late.

჻

NICK LOOKED AT HIS PHONE in dismay. When he had called AAA, it had been working.

The little signal scale at the top of his smart phone, was flat. The battery was dying. He should have plugged it into the car outlet. Before he turned off the engine.

And where <u>was</u> that tow truck? They should be here. He had planned to borrow the repairman's cell to call his prospective date.

Man, Delilah must be half steamed at you by now, he told his poor reflection in the windshield.

The light from his phone dwindled like in a B-rated zombie movie.

Dead battery.

With all that snow, the serviceman would never see him. Nick folded the coverlet over the passenger seat, covering the chocolates and a bouquet that looked sorrier by the minute. The red rose petals were already shriveling.

He cracked his door open, inviting a gust of cold inside the car that would kill the rest of the roses. He heaved himself half in, half out of the car, scanning the street for the flashing orange lights of salvation. Visibility had been reduced to a few feet.

Suddenly, a pair of yellow headlights pinned him down. A car approaching quickly, the driver bent on making his or her Valentine rendezvous in time.

Nick flattened himself against the snow-covered car. He sensed more than heard the tinny click as the speeding car doused him with filthy slush.

His gloved hand went to the latch.

Locked.

He brushed the window with his glove. His key was laughing at him from the ignition.

A brand-new car. An open invitation for any thief.

He should have taken the spare key with him. He should have bought the fancy button-key option.

Now he had locked himself out of his car. Could he get any unluckier? He hobbled along the valley building up from his bumper to the rear end of the parked car. His left leg struck the tow ball jutting out from the other car.

He fell face first in the snow. As he rushed to get back up, a nasty ripping sound told him his light coat had just gotten lighter. He fought the urge to kick the metal tow ball.

Then he tried the door of the passenger seat. Locked, too, the heart-shaped chocolate box and the wilting rose bouquet lying on the seat.

He bit his tongue in dismay. What an idiot he was.

Trusting a damn GPS, trusting a car salesman, trusting a shady agency, trusting the colleague who had suggested the shady agency.

He leaned his forehead against the roof, the word *Loser* fluttering about his head like a dark-winged Cupid.

This was the first time Nick had dared to enlist help for meeting *that special someone*. The agency counselor, a heavily made-up woman, had given pointers about buying a new car, getting some better clothes. She hadn't insisted on buying a membership in a gym, but her eyes kept going to his thickening waist.

That had been two months ago. After starving himself and splurging on a new car, Nick had made it a habit to climb the hundreds of stairs in the office building where he worked and had lost six inches and a meager twenty pounds. Nothing to change his mammoth silhouette.

He looked again, left and right. No flashing blue and orange lights.

He looked at the silver watch with its metal link wrist band. The towing service must be overloaded with calls.

He had the address on the GPS. He searched his internal memory drive and found the door number. There had been an apartment number, but he didn't remember it. But he would find her name on the lobby panel.

After a longing look at the gifts out of his reach, Nick zipped up his coat, and waddled off in the snow.

❧⸙

THE HEARTY VEGETABLE SOUP was cooling down. Dell had shut off the oven before the poor chicken burned. The gaudy yellow grandfather clock, a gift from Aline, ticked off the minutes toward her failure.

Two hours late.

She had an urge to call the guy. She punched his number, and after a tedious wait, got a "this-user-is-out-of-reach" message.

He must have seen the scar, she thought.

She touched her face. Such an ordinary, almost unremarkable incident.

The nervous tomcat Aline's toddler was playing with. Dell picking up the stray cat to prevent the baby from getting scratched. The stray, not happy, clawing, biting her. The subsequent infection, producing a permanent scar. Dell's insurance not covering fancy esthetic surgery.

Her stomach grumbled.

Finally, Dell resigned herself to a bowl of soup, that she had to re-heat in the less-than romantic microwave oven. She had shut off the Mozart-playing radio, a trait mentioned by her prospective date, who liked classical music.

She ate alone, in an eerie silence. The wind was not strong enough to whistle, and the snow was piling softly.

Because of the silence, Dell heard the front lobby door squeaking open. Was it possible?

She waited for the ding, her eyes locked on the metal intercom box flanking her door. But the visitor, whoever he or she was, did not ring the bell.

☙ ❧

HIS FEET WERE SOAKED through his Superior shoes. He had stepped into a puddle barely one hundred feet from his car. The metal handle of the zipper burrowed like a cold knife under his chin.

The temperatures were plunging; Nick regretted not having the emergency blanket with him. The blanket covering the gifts. At least he had the kid gloves, elegant, but useless against the biting cold.

He was tearing up, scanning the numbers going down through a fluffy snowfall. He should have put on real spectacles, instead of the contacts. When he passed the zero mark, dividing East and West, he felt the soaring joy of a marathon runner. He was heading in the right direction.

He crossed his arms, to place his gloved hands under his armpits. He had started the walk with his fists bundled in his front pockets. The relentless cold and the wind that had gradually picked up had frozen the tips of his fingers. He couldn't feel his toes.

Nick thought about the explorers, the First Nations who had lived there, with trees instead of the buildings. They had wintered in huts, without the comforts of electricity and engines. He had heard the stories of freezing temperatures and lost limbs.

He kept his mouth shut and kept walking. No open restaurants, no service stations along his way. The main artery would be running parallel to this street, on his left or right.

When he reached the 3000's after the zero divide, a tow truck emblazoned with the blue AAA logo sped past him, heading toward his dead car.

There and then, it felt like too much.

Just.

Too.

Much.

Nick reverted from a 34-year-old computer whiz to a two-year-old baby. He sat down in a snow bank and, hunched over, cried his heart out.

❧

DELL HAD ALMOST FINISHED HER SOUP. The noise bothered her subconscious mind. She walked mechanically over to her window like a prisoner making a familiar round.

The fresh snow had covered the path leading to the door.

Unmarked snow.

There should have been tracks left by whoever had entered the building. Maybe someone had gone out. She leaned her forehead against the glass, straining to see a receding silhouette. No tracks.

She heard a soft swishing, halting sound.

Then, if no one was entering, or exiting, that left…

"Oh, dear Lord!" she spat out.

Dell almost ripped out her dress bodice as she hurried to pull on a pair of purple yoga pants, leather boots and her heavy gray North Pole Goose Coat. She grabbed her keys and mittens as she rushed out of the flat.

She almost fell as she rippled down the wooden stairs, through the hall to the small lobby, and on to the main door, half opened.

Yes, there she was, lying half on, half off the path, the giant shovel cutting her in two.

"Mrs. Edwina!" she called, tears streaming down her face.

The lady's head swiveled, her knitted cap falling from her white hair.

"Oh, there you are, Delilah. Don't fret, I just took a spill."

Dell retrieved the cap, hoisted the frail owner up to her feet and guided her inside the lobby. As she sat Mrs. Edwina down on the faded blue sofa in the small lobby, Dell made sure she was not too shaken up.

"You should not be out shoveling," she chided her. "What if no one had seen you fall?"

A saying echoed in Dell's mind: *If a tree falls in the forest and no one hears it, does it make a sound?*

The older woman looked up at the tall brunette with kind blue eyes.

"I thought all you youngsters had gone out this evening."

"That's no reason for you to have a stroke."

Mrs. Edwina shook her head, her knobby hands clutched together.

"Oh, dear, you don't understand. Ever since my dear Marcus died, my nephew has wanted this building."

"To buy it?"

Dell thought it would be great for the owner to retire, as far from this winter as she could. Mrs. Edwina shook her bird-like head.

"No, Daniel wants to have me declared unfit and to take over the whole thing."

Dell pursed her thin lips. She had met that nephew, a major sleaze ball if she was any judge.

"So, if my nephew comes by and finds this path has not been cleared…"

Her voice trailed off. Dell understood the rest. *An unkept property, Your Honor. People could have tripped on their way in.* She had been asking Mrs. Edwina to hire help for some time, but maybe the old woman's finances were another sore point.

"I am so sorry," Dell said in earnest. "I should have come earlier instead of waiting for that stupid Valentine's day date!"

A hot tear slid down from her left eye, tracing a salty path all the way through her scar.

"You poor thing!"

Mrs. Edwina smiled.

"Say, what if I go make a nice cup of tea, so when you finish clearing the path you come have one?"

Having tea with the owner was not a habit, but Mrs. Edwina had never increased the rent since her husband had passed away. So, Dell nodded.

"Thank you. But don't hurt yourself."

Mrs. Edwina trotted gaily toward the apartment she had lived in for 55 years with her husband, and two years without him.

Dell set to work. The level of the snow had risen, and she had to push the door, tracing a thirty-degree slice in the snow to get out.

She checked the street no sleazy nephew in a dark Sedan in view. But then, visibility was so limited that she could only make out phantom blobs moving around.

She shoveled, putting all her pent-up anger into her work.

Doing something, at least, instead of waiting around like some stupid princess.

∽⚬∾

IN THE TIME it took Nick to walk along the avenue to the 4000s, the snow had piled up more than a foot high, shaped in rises and hollows by the wind. Visibility was so reduced that he could easily picture himself in a mountainous pass, braving the cold to catch up to his fur-clad brothers.

But he was a nerd, not some elfin warrior.

He plodded on, spent but strangely relieved.

His reserve of pride was depleted, and he decided to get to the place, present heartfelt apologies, and go.

A thousand street numbers later, he was walking like a zombie, all the feeling gone from his feet. His vision was more and more blurred. Maybe his eye balls were freezing inside his sockets. The snow was mocking his knees.

Maybe he wouldn't make it.

In this bleak, hollow landscape, that felt like a distinct possibility. He felt like a secondary character in a movie, not the sidekick, but the one left behind to die in the snow while the main cast plods on.

As soon as Nick got somewhere warm, a coffee shop, he would stop. He would ask very, very nicely, to make a phone call. At least, he could still feel the bulge of his wallet in the front pocket of his jacket.

As Nick was, for the nth time, looking about for a coffee shop, he noticed movement around a faintly lit entrance. He winced, to chase off the tears. It was the right street number, in dull bronze digits, set out by a lantern-like yellow lamp.

The parts of the grey or brown building he could see through the snowflakes showed age, and character. He stopped to look at the place.

He had expected some copy-paste block, all economic angles and sparse font railings.

This wasn't like that at all. He could follow the curlicues of the stone lintel, the bands of darker bricks, the diamond-shaped lighter ones. That four-story building, lean and mean, might hold eight to twelve apartments, unless there was an extension at the back he couldn't see.

It was the kind of older 1920s building like the one where little Nicky visited his maternal grandma for pastries, cookies and comics, so long ago. That this house had survived had him wondering.

His grandma's proud house had been reduced to rubble when Nick entered his teenage angst period, later supplanted by a twenty-story condo tower when he had landed his first programming gig.

In the soft cushion of freshly fallen snow, he could hear a sound out of place, grumbling and raging like that of a trapped animal. A hooded silhouette was battling a waist-high wall of snow pushed by the wind, gripping a shovel like a sword.

Nick couldn't see well because of the screen of snow flurries, except the heavy, no-nonsense, warm Everest-type coat the (*clerk? warrior monk?*) was wearing.

But he could hear the cursing through the wind

"Hey!" "Take that, you fiend!" "You bastard!"

The muffled voice uttering those curses was unmistakably feminine.

❧

DELL WAS MUTTERING UNDER HER BREATH and sweating profusely under the heavy North Pole coat. She should have put on a lighter one for this exercise.

She surveyed her progress. Less than she had hoped for. The sidewalk was a smooth white plain. That sneaky nephew could drive past at any time. She prayed that he was enjoying a very full and very long Valentine dinner.

Dell was getting tired. She had never tackled such a heavy snowfall on such short notice. And after a wasted evening spent fretting over a date.

"Need... a... hand?" a zombie-sounding voice asked from a short distance.

She turned, shovel at the ready.

A white mountain stood on the plain that had been the sidewalk.

A large man, covered with sparkling snowflakes. And under that layer of snow, God, he had no cap! She walked over to him, shovel in hand just in case, her yoga pants brushing snow aside.

He was wheezing and panting as if he had just run a marathon.

A full, 42.2 k one.

"Hum, are you sure you're OK?" Dell asked, afraid to see this Good Samaritan felled by a stroke at any moment. Or by sheer exposure.

The mountain man blinked, revealing a pair of cloud-grey eyes. A faint second rim revealed contact lenses.

He nodded, dislodging enough snowflakes to reveal how red his face was. And how his slick sports coat looked paper thin, and his soaked flannel pants even thinner. The knee-high snow hid his boots.

"Why, you're drenched!" Dell said, her voice muffled by her fur-rimmed hood. "You shouldn't…"

He shook his head, making more flakes fall. Then he extended a gloved hand.

Wordlessly, Dell let him take over her chore. Even if the mountain guy looked ill-equipped for winter, he shoveled the snow like a steam machine, huffing and puffing.

In five minutes he had cleared the path and was pushing snow out of the patch of sidewalk.

❧

THE EXERCISE PROVIDED NICK with a welcome occasion to vent his frustrations. He felt better bending, hoisting, pushing, throwing. Repeat.

From time to time he stole a look at the woman dressed for Mount Everest. Dark strands escaped from the large fur-trimmed hood; when she pushed her hair back inside, he saw a mark on her cheek, like a warrior's tattoo.

With the purple pants clinging to her legs, she looked like a high-fantasy heroine. A mountain elf warrior. Not the kind to wait by her window in a cocktail dress like his prospective date.

He threw a shovelful of snow with too much vigor. Poor Delilah. He would call her and tell her he was sorry.

As he was bending to push a shovel of heavy snow onto the street, a pair of pointy black boots entered his field of vision.

"What do you think you're doing?" a snarky voice asked.

Nick heard the sharp intake of air by the woman behind him. Fear?

"I'm, er, shoveling," he said, mustering his words.

The guy was standing in the patch he had just cleared on the sidewalk, wearing a leather jacket and baseball cap as unsuitable for this weather as Nick's own coat. The guy's face had this smart-assy quality he had often seen on the higher-ups in the corporate food chain.

The doofus had double-parked his car, and, if Nick's dulled senses did not betray him, the guy's Valentine date in the passenger seat was checking her make-up in a round hand mirror.

He turned his attention back to the guy. The smart-ass was smirking, but not at him.

At the Mount Everest woman.

ॐﳒ

OH, NO, NO, NO! Dell thought.

She should have talked to the nice stranger.

If the weasel nephew realized the voluntary nature of the work, it would be no better than finding the entrance filled.

There was only one way to save Mrs. Edwina.

"Oh, hi, Dan," she said with her best, innocent voice.

The mountain man and the nephew turned to her at the same time.

"Why, hel-loo! Miz Scarface," he drawled.

All her innards clutched in a tight knot at the nickname, a nickname gained after she had (politely) rejected his advances. Fury filled her. It was all so unjust!

But she had to think about gentle Mrs. Edwina. Dell took a deep breath. She would improvise, and hope that this nice stranger would catch on to her game.

"Mrs. Edwina says hello, Dan. By the way, she has hired Nick, here, to do the shoveling."

She had picked the first name that had come to her mind. Of course, the stranger froze, shovel in hands.

"Oh, really?" Dan said, turning to the man. "Nick who?"

"Nick Glass," she said, praying the stranger would forgive her later.

The mountain man shrugged.

"Yeah," he said, genially.

A wave of relief flooded Dell. Thank God for Good Samaritans!

Her happy feeling waned as she saw Daniel's face break into a too-wide smile.

"Well, let's see some ID here. I'm certain you won't mind, Miz Scarface, if I check who might be ripping off my aunt."

❧

HE HAD SEEN RIGHT THROUGH HER, Dell thought.

Dan would see another name on the ID card, and that would be that. She turned halfway to let her hood hide her tears.

The mountain man drew himself to his full height.

"Are you an officer?" he said in a rumbling voice.

In the cleared path, Dell noticed how drenched his… *shoes? fancy boots?* were. The coat was ripped.

"Because only an officer can force a free citizen to show his ID. You are aware of that, aren't you?"

"Well, you, big—" Daniel began.

Another voice piped in.

"Daaaan?" a voice called from a rolled down window of the double-parked car. "We're supposed to get to the *Stud Steak House!*"

"Jussa minute, hon'!" Dan said, impatiently.

He cranked his baseball-capped head up.

"I don't know what Miz Scarface told you, but…"

The mountain man moved so fast it was a blur. His paws clutched the lapels of Dan's leather jacket and his face was hovering close. When he spoke, it was a growl.

"Pal, first, if you really want to check my ID, you can call the police right now. Your double-parked car will be a boon for the first officer on the premises. And, second?"

He released Dan, pushing the nephew so hard that he landed on his bum in the snow bank.

"Her name isn't Scarface, it's DE-LI-LAH!"

❧

THE NEPHEW'S CAR DISAPPEARED in the whiteness, the engine's angry rumble dwindling into silence.

Once her own heartbeat had subsided, Dell walked over to her chocolate-less and flower-less Valentine date.

"I'm so sorry," they said in unison.

Then they exploded into an awkward babble.

"The GPS…" "Mrs. Edwina…" "East and West were so confusing…" "Locked out of my car…" "Had to clear the entrance…" "Phone dead…" "Didn't recognize your voice…"

"You said my n-name with s-such hope…"

Nick's voice was shaking from the cold seeping into his bones. He felt stupidly happy when Delilah took his arm.

"Let's get you inside before you turn into ice," she said. "Mrs. Edwina is making hot tea; I don't think she'll mind another guest. And we'll see about your car."

Her wide smile under the furred hood curled the Y scar on her cheek.

Yes, Nick thought, *she looked like a fantasy heroine*. One with a past, one with a story.

A story Nick was eager to learn.

THE END

Heartfelt Thanks

THIS BOOK IS THE BRAINCHILD of a writing exercise directed by Dean Wesley Smith. Dean asked us to write a short description of a character in a difficult situation. Nick and Dell sprouted fast!

Sheryl Curtis was nice enough to edit the text and correct my English. I claim for myself all remaining errors.

⊱⊰

LAST, BUT NOT LEAST, thanks to you, reader, for staying along for the ride. I hope you enjoyed the story. Feel free to share your enthusiasm with your friends and leave reviews on your favorite platforms.

About the Author

WHEN NOT TRYING to initiate first contact with strange flora, Michèle Laframboise juggles her time between drawing comics and crafting stories.

A science-fiction lover since childhood, she has written 17 novels and more than 40 short stories, earning three Auroras and two Solaris awards.

Her works have appeared in *Solaris, Carmilla, Galaxies, Géante Rouge, Brin d'Éternité, Tesseracts, Fiction River* and *Compelling Science Fiction.* She has been translated into French, Italian and Russian.

Holding degrees in geography and engineering, she uses her scientific background to create worlds filled with humor, invention and wonder.

Official website: www.michele-laframboise.com

Humoristic blog: sundayartist.wordpress.com

Publisher's website: www.echofictions.com

For some news and amusing reading reviews, join her merry band of readers:

http://michele-laframboise.com/fans

What does WOW means?

Wonderful Odd Women !

To know more about the WOW/Formidables collection:

Echofictions.com/collections/formidables

Other books by Michèle Laframboise

Change or die!

Science-fiction / humor / First contact /

Loongunis need constant fluctuations to thrive, while the strange-haired Earthmen hate the endless unstability.

When a sabotage impairs the shift engines of their traveling Box, the enforced immobility might drive all Loongunis mad...unless their translator can work out a solution!

Science fiction adventure at its best, a quirky 7000-word story told by multiple award-winning author Michèle Laframboise.

How to Think inside the Box
978-1-988339-40-5 (print)

Trapped in the most beautiful place on earth... What's a fearless birder to do?

Humor / mystery / Ornithology

Equipped with her Sibley Guide and trusty binoculars, Amanda Byrd pursues the most elusive winged species. As she explores a beautiful canyon at dawn, Amanda discovers their lift sabotaged, trapping their group at the canyon's bottom.

Who did it, and why?

Our intrepid birdwatcher must find a way out before the sun turns the canyon into a mortal cauldron.

A short and spirited cozy mystery introducing the energetic Lady Byrd, written by Michèle Laframboise, multi-award winner author and amateur ornithologist.

Condor Cliff

ISBN 978-1-988339-08-5 (Print)

You won't forget Malak...

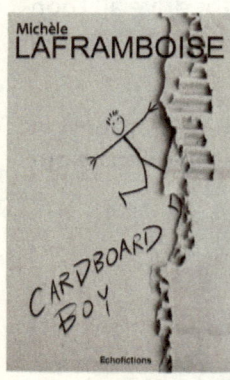

Child Labor/ Humanitarian / Sweatshops

Theo, a dispirited workplace humanitarian, audits a child worker at a cardboard factory, in a port city somewhere in Asia. He is impressed by young Malak's maturity and grit. When that boy, the same age as Theo's own son, disappears, he cannot let it rest. His quest for answers only raises more questions about the traps of structured help and acquired privilege.

An unsettling story quietly told by multiple awards-winning author Michèle Laframboise.

Cardboard Boy

ISBN 978-1-988339-22-1 (Print)

More books can be found at Echofictions.com !

Friends' list

A story links every reader in a chain of friendship.
Feel free to write your name before you give this book
to someone close.

This is a unique feature of the printed edition!

৯৵৹

_____

_____

_____

_____

_____

_____

_____

_____

_____

Yearning for more Stories?

You reached the last page, alas!

Michèle Laframboise's full bibliography is enough to whet any reader's appetite! Visit her author site at:

michele-laframboise.com

New stories are brewing up constantly!

To get exclusive offers, some curated book reviews, advanced information on events, join Michele's merry band of readers!

(michele-laframboise.com/fans)

As a very busy writer, Michèle won't send mail more often than once every two months.